This igloo book belongs to:

....

D0186313

igloobooks

Published in 2019
by Igloo Books Ltd
Cottage Farm
Sywell
NN6 0BJ
www.igloobooks.com

Copyright © 2016 Igloo Books Ltd
Igloo Books is an imprint of Bonnier Books UK

Illustrated by James Newman Gray
Written by Anne Marie Ryan

Designed by Jason Shortland
Edited by Natalia Boileau

0719 002.01
4 6 8 10 11 9 7 5
ISBN 978-1-78557-892-2

Printed and manufactured in China

Starlight Wishes

igloobooks

When the silvery moon shines
and we should be tucked up snug in bed,
we sit by our window
and dream of magic adventures instead.

We watch for an enchanted star,
shooting through the sky with a swish.
We imagine what we could do
if it granted our every wish.

Feeling so small, on a mountain so tall,
covered in sparkly snow,
we'd find a sled, all shiny and red
and shout, "Ready, steady… GO!"

Cold from our noses down to our toes,
we'd whoosh down the hill without a care.
Faster and faster we'd swoosh and slide,
swirling snowflakes in the air.

On a faraway desert island,
we'd be pirates brave and bold.
Wearing sailors' hats and a black eyepatch,
we'd dig deep for buried gold.

In the soft sand we'd find
an old treasure chest bursting at the seams.
It would be filled to the brim with precious
gems and jewels beyond our wildest dreams.

We'd whoosh up high,
right up to the sky.

Up and up we'd climb.

Zoooom!

We'd zoom down
fast with our hands
in the air, then do it
one more time!

On the back of a friendly dragon,
his scales shining in the sun,
we'd fly over a magical kingdom,
laughing and having fun.

Soaring over shining rivers,
we'd see tall, green shimmering trees.
Below would be a magic castle
and we'd swoop down on the breeze.

We'd slide down a sparkling rainbow
of orange and ruby red, too.
Sherbet yellow and gumdrop green
and beautiful, bright sky blue.

Indigo blue and zingy purple
would make us squeal with delight.
Then, POOF! We'd land in a big pot of
gold dust, sparkling in the light.

On candyfloss clouds we'd float
to a land where everything is sweet.
Marshmallow mountains and lollipop trees,
ready for us to eat!

There'd be houses made of gingerbread
and cakes filled with fluffy cream.
We'd gobble up all the tasty treats,
like the most delicious dream.

We'd fly to a land where stories come true,
in an enchanted wood.
Meeting Goldilocks, Cinderella
and Little Red Riding Hood.

Rapunzel would climb from her tower.
Beauty would wake in her bed.
We'd make lots of fairy tale friends
from the bedtime stories we'd read.

We'd zoom to the moon on our cosy beds
and see the earth below.
The stars would twinkle diamond bright
and the planets would softly glow.

Floating through the quiet blue,
we'd collect stars as we glided by.
Then, down and down we'd slowly drift,
through the deep, starry midnight sky.

Soon we'd be safely back at home, in the very best place of all.

In our snuggly little bedroom, we'd hang our stars up on the wall.

Starlight would shine all around
and remind us that wishes come true.
They whisk us to magical places
with lots of fun things to do.

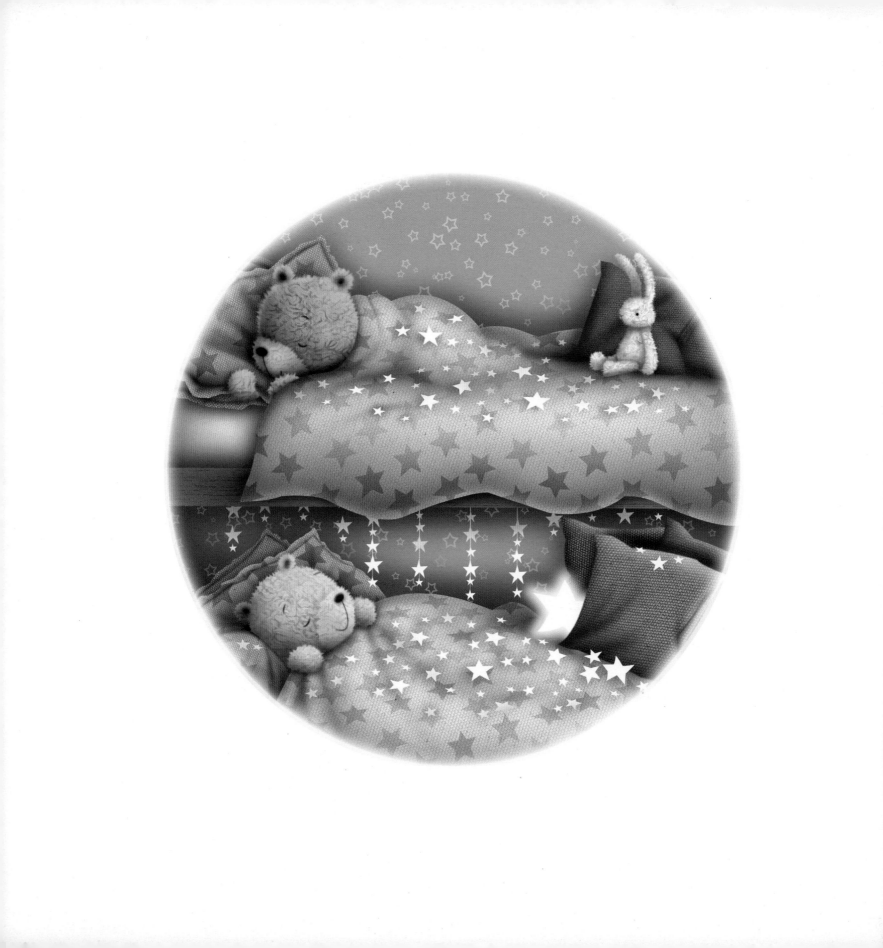